To my children who wanted chickens and ducks and my husband who was kind enough to say yes.

Tess Castro

Chicken Watching © Marites Castro 10/09/07

Children's 2ⁿᵈ Edition

Marites Castro
P.O. Box 445
Battle Ground, WA 98604

Beauty to Behold PhotoSeries ©Marites Castro 2007

Chicken Watching is a children's book. It is entertaining as well as educational. Are chickens smart enough to come knocking at the door? Do they form friendships? How do they handle conflicts?

Chicken Watching 2nd edition has three more stories: The Chicken and the Bunny, Chicken Leadership, and Where Do I Belong? They explore the questions: Do they know how to share? Do they have leadership? Do they accept others who are different?

Table of Contents

The First Egg

One day one of the chickens, Kellie, kept going in and out of the chicken coop. She was breathing hard. Then, she walked towards us and stayed by my daughter's feet.

My daughter petted her for twenty minutes. Later that day, Kellie laid the first egg. To our surprise, the color of the egg shell was blue.

Some of the chickens and ducks laid the blue eggs. Sometimes the egg had double yolks inside. The largest egg was laid by the duck and had double yolks.

Time-Out

Later on, we bought two baby chicks. We named them Estella and Miss Havisham. The two got along very well. Then five days later we bought two more chicks—Wendy and Bebe.

Wendy kept following Estella and Miss Havisham. She also liked standing in between the two. Miss Havisham did not mind Wendy tagging along, but Estella was not happy. Estella pecked Wendy a lot. To help her stop pecking, Estella was given a time-out.

Bebe, Wendy, Miss Havisham and Estella
Estella is cleaning Miss Havisham.

After the fourth time-out, Estella got a little better. Sometimes she looked like she was going to peck, but she stopped herself. After a while, she started pecking again.

So, she was given a longer time-out. After that she did not peck anymore. Ah, sometimes I, too, get grouchy and need a time-out to get used to changes around me.

Estella is pecking on little Wendy.

Estella is cleaning Miss Havisham. Wendy is standing between the two.

Wendy is the tag-a-long chicken.

Wendy is the smallest of all the chicks. She
just wanted to belong.

Estella and Wendy are getting along.

The Guard Chicken

Job Description:

Chicken needs to guard the strawberries and flowers from the bunnies.

Marianne took the job of a guard chicken.

The bunny was surprised to see Marianne.

Bunny: "What is this, a guard chicken?
I've never heard of such a thing."

Bunny: "Is that chicken for real?"

Marianne and the bunny are having a staring contest.

Marianne: "My human friend is watching us."

Bunny: "What should I do?
Think, think..."

Bunny: "Ah, the best bunny talent—multiply. Three bunnies against one chicken should do it."

Marianne: "Now what?"

The Chicken and the Bunny

Katherine: "This is my bunny friend, Roger."

Katherine: "There is a lot of food around here."

Roger: "Thank you for sharing."

Chicken Knocking At My Door

Katherine kept pecking too much and needed a time-out. We let her wander around the backyard away from the rest of the seven chickens. When it was getting dark, we heard a noise coming from the backdoor.

It was Katherine pecking and kicking the backdoor. Maybe she wanted to go back to the chicken coop to sleep. I wondered, "Is my chicken smart enough to come knocking at my door?"

Katherine: "I need a vacation from
the seven chickens."

Katherine: "The grass always looks greener on the other side."

Katherine: "It's getting dark.
It's time to go back to the chicken
coop and sleep."

Katherine: "I know the lady who takes care of us chickens is in there. I've seen her come in and out of this place. It's the human coop."

Katherine: "I don't think she heard me pecking the door. Maybe she will hear this— my karate chicken flying sidekick."

The Chicken and the Apple

Velma: "I don't think it is a forbidden fruit."

Velma: "It is here someplace."

Velma: "There it is."

Velma: "I don't think I can reach that high."

Velma is reaching for it.

Velma jumps for it.

The Karate Chicken

Captain Jack sometimes chased the chickens. The chickens kept a close watch on Captain Jack.

One day Emily and Captain Jack had a staring contest. We watched them stare at each other. After a couple of minutes, poor Captain Jack looked dazed, shook his head and walked away from Emily.

Captain Jack

Later on that day, Captain Jack walked back to stare at Emily again. Emily stared back and spread both her wings. She lifted one of her foot as if she was going to kick Captain Jack.

Her actions made us laugh. She reminded us of one scene from a movie called the Karate Kid. From that day on, Captain Jack did not chase or stare at Emily as much as the other chickens.

Emily is coming out of the chicken coop.

The Voice

We enjoyed listening to the chickens when they make sounds. It's their way of talking. Velma makes sounds that are lower and deeper than the other chickens.

One day Captain Jack came close to Velma and stared at her. Velma stared back and then made sounds in a very low and deep voice. Captain Jack was surprised by the low and deep voice. Captain Jack ran away from Velma.

Chicken Leadership

Kellie was the leader of the chickens. She walked around with Katherine most of the time. They pecked Emily and Velma a lot.

So, we gave them a time-out. Later on we put them back together. Katherine tried to peck Emily. Instead of pecking back, Emily stared at her. Katherine walked away.

Kellie tried to peck Velma. Instead of pecking back, Velma made a low deep sound. Kellie walked away.

When Kellie tried to peck Emily, Velma walked in between them and made a low deep sound. Kellie walked away.

Later on, Velma became the leader of the group. She used her voice instead of pecking at the other chickens and ducks.

Velma is enjoying the grass with the other chickens and ducks.

Where Do I Belong?

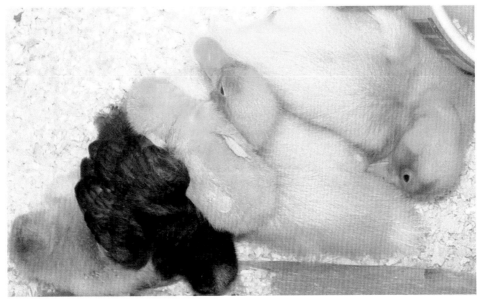

We bought three chickens and two ducks. We named them Marshmallow, Spots, Buffy, Mandy, and Ichigo.

When they were about two months old, we took them out to be with the other chickens and ducks. The three chickens started to walk around with the other chickens. The two ducks started to walk around with the other ducks.

Most of the time, Marshmallow, Buffy, and Spots walked around together. A month later, Buffy and Marshmallow died. I wondered, "How will this affect Spots? Who will she walk around with?"

Spots started to walk around with the other chickens but the other chickens were not used to her.

Front: Mandy, Mudpie, Courtney Back: Ichigo

Later, she started walking with the ducks she grew up with—Mandy and Ichigo. The other ducks, Courtney and Mudpie, were not used to have Spots walking with them.

To our surprise, Mandy and Ichigo protected Spots whenever the other ducks and chickens tried to peck her. I wondered, "Where does she really belong, with the chickens or with the ducks?"

My husband said, "Maybe she belonged to both. She is a chicken duck—a chuck." We laughed at his made-up word. Perhaps, he is right. So, we nicknamed her "Chuck."

The Chicken Herder

Seth, our dog, sometimes helps us herd the chickens back to the chicken coop.

Spots is keeping a close watch on Seth.

The chickens are enjoying the apple tree.

Made in the USA
San Bernardino, CA
12 June 2018